Filthy: Hot & Dirty Sex Stories

Erotic Short Stories for Women

Vivienne Dupont

Table of Contents

Sex with a stranger in the elevator

And then he grabs me, presses me against the wall, kisses me while his hand wanders deeper and deeper. I feel his hot breath on my neck, his fingers on the hem of my skirt and his hard bulge pressing against my legs. I can hardly wait for him to finally turn me over and fuck me properly.

But what is that noise? That penetrating beeping?

Can it stop?! Hot stranger gets off me all of a sudden. He hears the beeping, too.

"What are you doing? Why aren't you getting up?" he asks suddenly and I stare at him, confused.

How? I'm standing. How am I supposed to get up?

I look down at myself. Suddenly I'm no longer wearing my white blouse, which I put on today without a bra, and also no longer the tight skirt that hasn't really fit me for years, but instead: an old pair of pyjamas. The one with the little black glitter stars.

How embarrassing!

And suddenly it's no longer the hot brown-haired guy standing in front of me, but my unattractive, fat boss. What's happening?!

"You're late again," my boss says suddenly.

I wake up and take a deep breath. It was all just a dream. Unfortunately. Or fortunately. I'm not quite sure.

I turn off my alarm clock, want to turn around again and try to dream myself into the stranger's arms, but then I turn around again in a panic. What was that I just read? 7:30?

Oh shit!

I'm really late!

I quickly jump up, run into my bathroom and turn on the shower. While the water runs slowly warm, I peel myself out of my star pyjamas and stand under the hot water.

In record time I shower, brush my teeth, put on my clothes and slap some more makeup on my face.

Completely out of breath, I grab another banana in the kitchen and then run to the train.

If she's on time, so am I. But of course... she's late. Damn!

Impatiently I step from one foot to the other. Not today of all days! Not today, when I have that important meeting with a client. Oh, boy!

The train arrives, I squeeze into the full compartment and pray that no other unforeseen incident happens.

But fortunately, it doesn't happen.

I run into the office and make it to the conference room just in time.

"Ah, Mrs. Stefan. Just in time," says my boss as he is about to close the door.

Completely exhausted, I settle down on one of the chairs, inconspicuously try to wipe the sweat from my face and almost choke on the water, which I drink in one go.

What a messy morning!

But luckily I manage to get through the presentation with aplomb and even get invited to lunch with the potential clients and my boss. That sounds promising.

Completely finished with the nerves, I go to the toilet rooms and do not even listen when the colleague calls me something. I don't care what it is. It won't be more important than the few minutes of rest I'm about to allow myself.

I come back and notice that I have neither paper nor pens at my place and make myself again to go to our reception, where usually always a few office utensils are to be found. But Nadine is not sitting in her place and I daren't just look in the cupboards.

I take a look down the hallway which I can see through the glass door and see my the colleagues standing outside my office, waiting for me to come back. But I figure they can wait a little longer. I'm still completely under power and would love to go straight to lunch. But unfortunately it's still an hour too early for that.

So I decide I'll go to the basement to provide paper supplies myself.

I press the button of the elevator and hear the sound behind me that tells me that an elevator is just stopping at my floor. What luck!

It's almost empty, too, which is why I scurry in.

"Hello," I murmur to the man who must work on one of the upper floors and whom I've never seen before. But how could I. The office building is huge and as often as the companies change here, it's impossible to know all the people here.

But he doesn't pay any attention to me and stares at his mobile phone. Through the mirrored walls in the elevator I can look directly at him. A typical suit wearer. However, his suit fits pretty well and also suits him. His dark brown hair is combed back with a lot of gel. But it doesn't look stupid. It actually looks pretty good, just as he looks good. Outrageously good, to be honest.

Now I'm even more annoyed that he didn't even return my "hello". Stupid, arrogant pretty boy! Then I'm not going to say "bye" to you anymore and I'm not going to wish you a nice day like I usually do.

I wait for us to stop at the ground floor and for him to disappear again, but somehow that doesn't happen. The elevator stops moving and suddenly it jerks. Startled, I hold onto the stranger and immediately pull my hands back when the jerking stops.

Irritated, he looks first at his arms where my hands had just been and then at my face.

Whew! What beautiful light blue eyes.

"Sorry. Reflex!" is all I say as I realize what I've just done. You're still allowed to cling to something when the elevator jerks, right? Tz!

But why does it jerk at all? And why won't it go any further? The question is much more important.

I press the buttons, first the open button, then to the ground floor and the basement. But nothing happens.

"Mhh," I murmur, slowly wondering if the stranger just doesn't feel like talking to me or if maybe he's mute.

But then his cell phone rings and he answers it. It was probably just because he didn't want to speak. Arrogant guy!

"I'm still in the elevator. Be right down," he says, then impatiently presses the "EG" button. But still nothing moves.

I see him looking at me through the mirror.

"Mhh," he does now too, looking at me questioningly.

I just shrug my shoulders. No idea what's going on here right now.

Once again I press all the buttons, but nothing happens.

I see the stranger roll his eyes in annoyance. Yeah, I don't like it here either! He pulls out his cell phone again and calls the person who is probably waiting for him downstairs.

10

"The elevator's stuck. It's gonna be a while. Sorry... no. I'm not alone? Oh, any of the offices downstairs," he says.

'Any one of the offices downstairs. I think he means me. And with that I now know what my colleagues mean when they talk about the "snobs" from the top floors. Of course, they have the best view, the most money and, in their opinion, the better jobs. I never understood why they were so hated, but I'm starting to get it. They really do seem to think they're better than everyone else.

I see him look at me and then nod.

Then he hangs up and shares a word with me for the first time.

"The elevator is broken and shouldn't have been used at all. However, I was so busy this morning and my assistant is sick that I didn't get the message regarding this," he says.

An assistant. Oh, great. Even my boss doesn't have one.

I'm trying to remember my morning. I didn't read a single email that was in my inbox. How could I? I haven't sat at the laptop for a second.

And I successfully ignored the words of my colleagues earlier.

I imagine I heard something like, "Elevator broken... don't use it." I wasn't sure earlier. Besides, it was working. Well... until just now.

"And now?", I ask. After all, he has a cell phone in his hand and could call for help.

"The repair company is already on the way. But it's going to take some time. Why didn't you know not to use the elevators?"

"I've been busy as well. Hectic morning," I reply curtly.

I can feel him still looking at me. My God.

It should be illegal to dress so disturbingly well. No wonder he's so successful. How could anyone say no to him?

I see him sit down on the floor. I wouldn't have expected that. His fabric is crumpling and his suit is getting dirty. It must have cost a lot!

"I guess it'll be a while," he says, grinning at me.

Okay. Take it easy. He's only human. Not a god or anything.

Suddenly I feel that I want to sit down too. My feet hurt. I always have a pair of fancy pumps stashed in my office for important appointments. Today was one of those appointments. That's why I'm wearing them. I've never had them on for more than two hours at a time, though. They look good, but they're terribly uncomfortable. My toes are starting to go numb.

I also sit down and try to be as elegant as possible. It would be a nightmare should my skirt tear at this moment - it is damn tight.

I notice how he has been watching me and inwardly pat myself on the back for not making any nonsense of it. I lean my back against the wall, stretch out my legs and cross them. All very elegant.

He hasn't taken his eyes off me and I notice now that he's no longer looking at my face, but staring at my legs.

Did I not shave them or something? I follow his gaze and I see nothing. No stubble, no dirt, nothing. They actually look very nice. I treated them with a very rich moisturizer last night, so they're still nice and shiny today.

So why is he staring at them like that?

Confused, I look at him and then our eyes cross.

"Sorry. I was just admiring how neat your legs look."

Oh. Okay.

"Very pretty," he adds, and I feel myself blush. No one could have expected that!

He looks away again and glances nervously at his mobile phone. I've completely lost track of time and don't know how long we've been stuck in here. Five minutes? Ten? Half an hour?

"I guess my next appointment starts without me," he says, shrugging.

He seems more relaxed than before. He's probably resigned to being stuck here in the elevator with me for the rest of the day.

"At least I'm stuck here with you and not one of my colleagues," he then tells me with a grin.

How? He favors me? How can that be?

I just grin and don't even know what to say to that. He's just so outrageously good looking. I hardly dare to look at him.

Then suddenly he curses and I have to look up.

"Mm?", I inquire.

"I just got a text from my colleague who is waiting for me downstairs at the entrance. He got the information that it can still take a few hours."

"A few hours?", I ask in shock.

"Yes. The technicians are there. But it's probably a bigger problem that they can't fix without special equipment. They're pretty annoyed that we're here, too. After all, they announced they were coming yesterday. " He shrugs his shoulders innocently.

It's actually our fault that we're stuck here now. I wish I'd listened when my colleagues were talking to me earlier. But, here we are.

I start the change my seating position, it seems like I need to get comfy if we're in here for the long haul. My feet are hurting so much. Uncertainly I look aroundI wonder if I can just take off my pumps?

I look at him and notice that he has his head propped against the wall and his eyes closed. Is he asleep? Well, then he certainly doesn't notice me taking off my shoes.

Carefully, I slip out of my pumps and immediately notice the relief as I stretch them and briefly massage them with my hands.

"They look really uncomfortable. I really wonder how you girls can stand to be on them for just one day," he says suddenly, and I wince. He's seen it after all. Crap.

I just grin innocently.

"You get used to it," I finally reply.

"Well ... it looks pretty good." He opened his eyes again and grins at me.

I need to take a deep breath. He's really driving me crazy.

As if in a trance, I reach for my feet. I usually do this when I have taken off my shoes, so that I can give my tired feet a quick massage. I quickly knead them until I feel the relief and can move them in all directions again.

"May I help you with that?" the handsome stranger says suddenly.

Excuse me? Help with what? Confused, I look around. Maybe the techs got in unnoticed, but no. It's just the two of us now. And sure enough, he's looking at me. Me and my feet.

He sees my astonishment and then points to my feet.

He really wants to help me with that?

Speechless, I lift up my right foot, which he then grabs and starts massaging.

His hands are dexterous and it does real good. Still, I find the whole thing very absurd. First the compliment. Now the massage. What comes next? A kiss? Sex?

Carefully he works on my right foot, puts it carefully back on the floor and then takes care of the left one.

Continuing to watch him speechless, I murmur a soft "thank you" as he finishes.

"Those are really nice feet," he finally says, his gaze wandering back and forth between my face, my legs, and my feet.

"Thank you," I say again and now I don't even know how to act. I'm suddenly hot and I feel that there's something in the air. He doesn't just do that like that.

Suddenly he stands up and moves. He settles down right next to me and grins at me from the side.

"You know what?" he starts a conversation.

"I've often imagined what it would be like to get stuck in an elevator. I'm sure you know what that's like. You always secretly hope that when you're alone in it with an attractive person. I was wishing the same thing when I saw you earlier. And for some reason, I got my wish."

What?!

I'm completely confused. He barely looked at me before. Why would he think that?

"Yeah, sorry. I always come off as standoffish at first. But that 'make yourself scarce and seem aloof when you're attracted to someone' thing, it's not just women who can do that. I do it too. Unfortunately," he explains.

I still don't know what to make of that. Confused, I look around. Maybe there are hidden cameras somewhere. But even if there are, I don't know what something like that should look like.

So I turn my attention back to him. He continues to look at me and then he moves his hand. It's on my leg now. On my bare leg, because my tight skirt has slipped up.

Astonished, I stare at his hand, which he quickly pulls away.

"Sorry," he says, raising his hand.

"I guess that was a little too forward."

He probably isn't used to a woman not jumping on him right away. But if it wasn't so absolutely absurd, I wouldn't hesitate for a second.

On the other hand ... what's going to happen?

We make out, maybe we actually have sex here in the elevator, and even if I never see him again after that, I still would have had sex in an elevator with an astonishingly hot guy. Could be worse, right?

"No, it's fine," I finally say, putting his hand back on my leg. Besides, it felt pretty good.

"Oh, how nice," he replies with a grin, moving his hand. He starts stroking my leg and then keeps moving upwards until it eventually reaches the hem of my skirt.

I turn my face in his direction and he comes closer to me. His other hand grabs my head and then he kisses me.

Wow ... it's like a kiss in a movie. The protagonist finally kisses her Prince Charming at the end, who she's been adoring for the previous 90 minutes. Except he's not really my Prince Charming. But at least he looks like it.

Everything tingles and it's one of those kisses where you automatically close your eyes because it feels so good.

19

He lets go of my face again and looks at me with a grin.

I grin back and unceremoniously swing myself wide-legged onto his lap. There's no turning back now anyway and why shouldn't I arrange this the way I like it best?

He grabs me and automatically my skirt pushes up. I feel his hands on my body. First on my waist, then on my butt and then on my bare legs until he puts them back on my bare ass. It's a good thing I opted for the skimpy panties this morning and not the love killer.

His grip gets stronger as he reaches my bottom. He holds it tight, kneads it and kisses me more and more intensely.

God, how good that feels. How I've missed this.

I run my fingers through his hair, really grab and become wilder and more uninhibited. I desperately want to feel him inside me.

I slide back a little on his floor and start unbuttoning his pants. He is wearing a belt, which I also undo and then pull down the zipper. I can already see his hard bulge through the fine suit fabric and reach for it through his blue boxers.

He moans in my ear as my fingers touch his hard spanking and helps me pull it out.

He is big, thick and incredibly hard. With pleasure I massage him with my hand while he pushes my skirt a little further up and reaches between my legs with his fingers. He pushes the fabric of my panties aside and starts to work my pussy. Skillfully and intensely he rubs my clit until I cling to his shoulder and moan into his ear.

Then he slides a finger into my wet hole and starts fucking me with it.
My God, if he keeps this up, I'll come in no time.

He loosens his grip and I look up in surprise. Why has he suddenly stopped?

He grabs me by the waist and pushes me back first onto the floor. Then he spreads my legs, licks once over his full lips and pulls my panties aside again before he disappears with his head between my legs.

I moan out loud as I feel his tongue on my pearl.

Oh, man. Not only with his fingers he is skillful, but also with his tongue. He licks me first very slowly and with a wide tongue and then he sharpens it to tease my clit. He does this alternately until he pushes two fingers deep into my pussy and presses them right against my G-spot.

Phew ... I've totally forgotten where I am by now. Have blanked out everything around me. I just focus on his fingers and on his tongue and then I come. And how.

I moan, let out my lust and lie there completely breathless and speechless.

Slowly, he pulls back and grins at me.

I see his cheeks flush and his cock continue to stick up steeply.

I collect myself for a moment and then straighten up. Now it's his turn.

I reach for his hard cock, jerking it with my hand before I go down with my head and touch it with the tip of my tongue. I taste his first drops before I then take his cock deep in my mouth.

I hear him start to moan. Feel his hands on my head and continue. Let my tongue wander over his shaft, play with its tip, before I then push it deep into my throat.

"Oh madness," I hear him say just before I pull the spanking back out.

"Fuck me," I say, looking at him intently.

I straighten up and hold onto the wall of the elevator with my hands, then push my skirt way up and let my panties slide to the floor.

I present my bare ass to him while looking at him over my shoulder.

Immediately he gets up and stands behind me. His hands he puts on my hips and then he leads his cock to my pussy. I feel him slide it through my wet crack once and then he thrusts hard. I moan out as I notice him penetrating me deeply.

Oh, how good that feels.

He holds me tight as he starts fucking me with hard, deep thrusts.

I hold onto the handles of the elevator and enjoy the way it takes me from behind.
His hands bury themselves in my hips and then I feel a firm slap on my ass. I groan out loud. Just what I needed right now.

He feels me groan in pleasure and my body twitches. Once again he slaps my ass with the flat of his hand and one more time I moan loudly.

He fucks me further and becomes faster and harder. I notice how the next climax is approaching.

"Harder. Faster," I cheer him on and he immediately does what I tell him.

He speeds up, his cock drills deeper into me, and then I cum again.

I can also hear him moaning louder and louder. Once again he accelerates his pace.

"I'll be right there," I hear him murmur. He thrusts hard a few more times and then he comes too.

Completely out of breath he holds me tight and tries to calm down again. I feel how fast his heart beats and also the last twitch of his cock shortly before he pulls it out of me again.

He turns me around once more, grabs my face and kisses me one more time before we fix our clothes and sit back on the floor.

His hand is on my leg as he glances at his phone.

"Oops. Five missed calls," he says, dialing the number that just tried to call him.

"Oh, wonderful. Yes, see you in a minute," I hear him say.

"The techs are there, working on getting us out of here. We should be free in a few minutes," he finally says when he hangs up.

Relieved, I slowly straighten up and look into the mirrored walls of the elevator. My make-up and my hair are a little out of place and I try to save a little of it.

He also stands up and looks in the mirror. I have tugged quite firmly at his hair, which is now all messed up. Grinning, he tries to fix it too and then puts his jacket back on.

We look at each other once more, kiss and only a few seconds later the elevator starts moving again.

We stop on the ground floor and the doors open again.

A few of my colleagues, my boss, the technicians and his colleagues stand in the foyer and look at us pityingly.

"Oh you poor things. I hope it wasn't too bad," my colleague says, taking me in her arms. As if I needed consolation now...

He is also received and I can see him silently calling out to me "see you soon" as well as a particularly wide grin as he turns and gets into the already waiting car.

I get the rest of the day off to recover from this dramatic and...shall we say...interesting experience!

Sex with my best friend

"And then what happened?", Andi, my best friend, wants to know from me.

"Then what happened? You mean after he penetrated me and came, like, right away? Then nothing happened at all. He rolled over and went straight to sleep."

Andi snorts and laughs.

"What, what a loser!" he yells.

I nod.

"Yes, I woke him up then and sent him straight home. If he doesn't even bother to make me come as well, then surely I'm not going to make sure he has breakfast the next morning. Or put up with me not being able to sleep all night because he snores terribly. Of course he was totally pissed off that he now had to drive home in the middle of the night. But I didn't care. I never want to see him again anyway."

"Oh wow. That must have been quite an experience," he says compassionately.

I nod vigorously. And it really did start off so well.

I met Stefan a week ago at a party. We flirted a lot, even kissed, but only innocently. He didn't even want to give me a French kiss and was quite reserved. I figured he was doing that as his way to hold back, because he is looking for the great love and not just sex.

We exchanged numbers and arranged to go for a walk and eat ice cream a few days later. There followed again only a sweet little goodbye kiss.

And then the date last night. Man, was I excited. He invited me to dinner, to a restaurant near me. We hit it off, and then we decided to go back to my place... For a glass of wine. I knew it wouldn't last, of course. I shaved extensively beforehand and put on my nicest underwear. And then we started. We kissed on the sofa. He was again very timid. Only ever kissed me on the mouth with his lips closed. Neither put his hands on my waist nor on my face. It was so completely ... emotionless. But I figured maybe that would change once he warmed up. So I took off my clothes and presented him with my pretty lingerie.

Then he actually woke up and became more active. He kissed me again, caressed my body and also

28

undressed. Everything, you know, everywhere, was really very handsome, even though he didn't put as much effort into grooming as I did. He had a real bush down there. I still thought to myself that he certainly didn't expect me to sleep with him today and was able to see past that. Normally I don't like that at all.

We are then in my bedroom and have laid down on my bed. Well, and then the drama began.

He then grabbed my head and I was starting to think he was finally going to get a little more passionate and kiss me really hard right away, but he tried to push it down instead. To give him a blowjob. Pfft - figures.

I just said no. I had no desire to have his hair in my mouth and have put off him to the next time.

Then I thought maybe he was doing it to me. After all, I put extra effort into my shave. But, nothing. He just touched me there briefly and then climbed over me, jerked his cock and then fucked me.

Well... you can't call it fucking. He penetrated me. He moved minimally and then came.

And that was it. He gave me a kiss on the cheek, turned away and closed his eyes.

I, of course, lay there completely perplexed and didn't know what to do.

Is that it? Is this his idea of good sex?

"Can you maybe turn off the lights?" he asked me then.

I then jumped up and freaked out a bit. I asked him whether he should not still take care of me and whether he thinks that was just really good?!

Then he asked me in all seriousness: whether I had not also come!

How in the world did he think I was gonna get off from five seconds of sex?!

"But I stroked you, too, and then you moaned," he said.

Yeah. Oh, my God. I moan when I'm hot for a guy and he touches me for the very first time. But that's not moaning during an orgasm.

Anyway, I then promoted him from my apartment and deleted his cell phone number immediately. I really don't want to deal with such morons. My time is too valuable for that.

"You really have no luck with men," Andi brings me back from my thoughts.

Unfortunately, he's right about that. My relationship just before failed after I caught the asshole with a

30

friend of mine. I ended the relationship immediately. The friendship too, of course.

I didn't want a long mourning period and started dating again right away. He's stolen enough years from me already, I'm not going to let another day go by to cry over him.

But somehow the men after that were all nothing. The first one was married and forgot to tell me about it. Please, how can you forget such a detail when you meet someone new?

The second one was great in bed, but totally unreliable. I don't know how many times he stood me up and how many times I let him get away with it. But the last time was then once too much. There I was sitting at home after a really exhausting day and actually prepared to go into the bathtub and enjoy a glass of wine. But he wanted to go celebrate with me. So I picked myself up again after he really spent a lot of time trying to talk me into it. Shaved, put on makeup and got dressed up and just when I was done with everything and waiting for him to pick me up, he lost his phone, crashed it or whatever. Because he just didn't answer me again. Not until the next day. That's when he apologized and said that a buddy stopped by his place and wanted to have a drink with him. Something turned into a lot and in the end he forgot about me and went off on his own. Well, thanks a lot!

And then the last one ... the fast comer.

"Don't you think the next time would have been better?", Andi asks me.

Energetically, I shake my head.

"It's not like there's a problem with being early. Not at all. But it is a problem when you don't understand the problem. That you just assume that sex is over now and you can sleep now. But that one couldn't even kiss really well. What did I expect!", I retort and throw my hands up. Bad kissers have never been good in bed. That should have been a warning to me.

"Now what?" asks Andi.

I shrug my shoulders.

"Now you need to get drunk with me and we'll go," I finally say.

"Good plan!" He pulls the cork off the wine bottle and fills both glasses.

"Cheers!" he says, and we toast.

I feel the wine moistening my throat and the alcohol slowly going to my head.

And then I just remember the two of us screeching like two teenagers as we got out of the cab to run to the nearest club.

We've both been over 30 for a few years now, but being single over 30 still makes you feel like you're 18. We danced our hearts out, drank shot after shot, and at one point we were completely wiped out sitting on one of the couches that were in a dark corner in the club.

The sofa was actually big enough for both of us, but then suddenly a totally drunk girl around 18 sat down with us because she was so dizzy and needed to rest for a minute.

So of course we didn't say no and slid in close together. And then somehow it happened. His hand was on my leg. Probably totally unnoticed and accidental. Where else are you supposed to grab his hand when you're sitting shoulder to shoulder squashed against each other. But then we both looked at his hand and grinned. Our faces got closer and closer and then we kissed.

Maybe just to see what it's like. We've never done this before. We've known each other so long, we never thought about it. Besides, I was always in a relationship. And when it was over, the friendship with Andi felt more like a friendship between two women. After all, he knew everything about me and my problems.

But the kiss was good. It felt right. He's definitely one of the really good kissers. I wonder if he's as good in other areas.

That must have been what I was thinking when I suggested we could go again. To me.

And now we're sitting next to each other in silence in the cab. I think he knows exactly where this is going and he didn't say no. That's a good sign, right? But is it really such a good idea?

On the other hand ... what have we got to lose? Our last relationships failed because we didn't know our partners as well as we always thought we did. We both know each other inside and out. If that should work out right away and we also harmonize with each other in bed, that would be the jackpot.

"We're here," Andi says and pulls out his wallet to pay the taxi driver. Then he opens the door and waits for me. I get out and reach for his hand, which he holds out to me.

He pulls me to him and we face each other again. His face comes closer and closer to mine and then we kiss again. First very gently, but over time more wild and stormy. I can feel how his lust is growing and I feel the same.

Hastily we walk to my front door, I unlock it and we run through the stairwell to my apartment.

No sooner have I unlocked the door and switched on the light than our clothes fall to the floor. First the jackets, then the shoes and on the way to my bedroom the rest.

Still dressed only in his underwear, he grabs me and pushes me onto my bed.

Andi knows exactly what I like. How often have I told him about it.

He kisses me again and then wanders with his mouth over my body. First he nibbles on my neck, before he gently bites into it. His hands are on my breasts, he kneads them and gently takes them out of the cups of my bra. He now turns his attention to my nipples, which are already sticking out hard. With his mouth he sucks on them before he carefully bites and nibbles on them.

Then he unbuttons my bra and flings it to the floor before returning his attention to my body.

With his mouth he wanders over my belly down to between my legs.

I'm wearing skimpy briefs - the kind where you can just push the fabric to the side, which he does now.

His fingers run through my wet cleft and press right down on my clit.
Momentarily, I groan.

Now if only he knows that I like to be licked while two or three fingers are inside me, I'm sure I'll come a time or two today.

And then I feel them. His fingers on my wet hole. They circle it and then push in very slowly. He starts fucking me with them. Very slowly and carefully until he pushes them in deep and searches for my most sensitive spot.

He found it, pressing against it again and again as he continued to lick my clit.

Oh, man. I'll be right there.

He continues. Fucks me with his fingers while his tongue presses on my clit.
My fingers claw into the bedspread and my entire body tenses. I have my eyes closed and focus only on the good feeling and then I come. Quivering with bliss.

Very slowly Andi lets go of me again. Pulls his fingers carefully out of me and then strokes very gently over my body while I let the orgasm fade.

For a few minutes I just lie there while my heart beats wildly and my breathing slowly calms down.

"Are you okay?", I hear him ask.

Immediately I nod. And notice how well I'm doing!

I straighten up and now push him onto the bed. He's still wearing his boxers, which are already suspiciously baggy. I pull them down and I am very impressed. I've never seen Andi naked. In his underwear, yes, or once in a bathing suit, but not completely naked yet. Especially not with a hard-on. I never expected him to be so well endowed.
With pleasure I run my hand over his hard cock. Just how I like it.

Then I hold him tight and go down with my head. I play with my tongue on his glans. Lick it, suck on it, before I take his spanking then in my mouth.

I hear him start to moan. His hands gently rest on my head and guide me ever so slightly. I bend back and forth while sucking his cock.

His breathing quickens, his moans louder.

"Stop it or I'll be right there," he mutters, and in wonderment I stop.

"I don't want to come yet," he then adds, pulling me to him so he can kiss me.

I land on top of him as he holds me down with his arms, sitting me down on his legs as they rub his cock.

Gently, I move back and forth and hear him start to moan again.

He grabs me by the waist, lifting me briefly, only to have me sit down on his stiff spanking.

I feel him penetrating me and slowly filling me. I moan briefly in pleasure as he is completely inside me.

Mhh ... how good that feels.

He continues to hold me by the hip and thus determines the pace. Sometimes a little faster and then again a little slower to enjoy it. I tense my legs and let go again.

But then he lifts me up again and we turn. My back is now on the bed. He is above me. He spreads my legs and then lifts them. Again he penetrates me as he puts my legs on his shoulders. This makes him come even deeper.
I enjoy every single thrust and feel myself about to come again.

He takes my legs off his shoulders again, holds me by the ankles and fucks me harder now.

With my hand I now start to rub my clit. I do not need a minute, and come again.

My body twitches and my pussy tightens around Andi's cock. I see how he closes his eyes, gets faster and faster and then also comes loudly.

He puts my legs back on the mattress and takes one deep breath.

He then opens his eyes again and beams at me.

"That was better than I expected," he admits, then lies down next to me to give me a tight hug.

I couldn't agree more. I don't know when the last time someone was so responsive to me.

We notice how tiredness suddenly overtakes us and quickly fall asleep.

When I wake up in the morning slightly hungover, but otherwise with a clear head, Andi is of course still lying next to me and suddenly I panic.

I don't know why I let you do this to me. You don't do that to your best friend!

But when he wakes up as well and grins at me, I know this wasn't a mistake and our story will definitely continue ....

A cuckold with my husband

'm standing in our bedroom going through our wedding album again. It's been 10 years since I married the love of my life and I couldn't be happier. We fight every now and then, of course, but we make up every time and it's like nothing happened.

I met my husband Thomas over 15 years ago. It was right on my first day at University. I moved to another city and didn't know anyone, of course.

That's why I was standing all alone in front of the lecture hall where the introductory meeting was about to take place and I was really nervous. I remember that I was totally unsettled by the fact that most of the students had already formed groups.

But then there was Thomas. He, like me, was also alone and smiled shyly at me when our eyes crossed.

I was instantly blown away when I looked into his blue eyes and watched him brush his blonde strands out of his face with his fingers.

I returned his smile and then he walked up to me.

"Are you here all by yourself too?" he asked me. I was much too shy to answer with many words and just nodded.

We then sat down next to each other and since that moment we have been inseparable. We studied together for university, ate together in the canteen and explored the city together. Like me, Thomas moved here from another city and didn't know anyone else.

But it actually took over a year before we kissed for the first time. I remember it very clearly. We were at a party and although I had a little crush on Thomas from the start, we pretty quickly clarified that we were just friends.

He had a girlfriend and I had a boyfriend. But for some reason, which I don't even know anymore, Thomas and I broke up with our partners and went to the party as singles.

We had already drunk quite a bit and at some point he said that it would be totally easy if we were both a couple. After all, we have the same interests, the same sense of humor and can really tell each other everything without the other judging. I just nodded and thought how absurd that would be. But then he kissed me. And that kiss changed everything. It sounds totally cheesy, but it was like a swarm of butterflies had always been dormant inside me and now they were about to erupt.

He was also totally overwhelmed and we spent the rest of the party making out. Really just making out. Nothing more.

He then came with me to the dorm and we fell asleep cuddling. We had sex only a week later and then we were firmly together.

We finished college together, got an apartment, and after we both found secure jobs, he proposed.

We got married in a fairly small circle, but we really splashed out on our honeymoon and treated ourselves to a wickedly expensive holiday in Bali. That was ten years ago and I couldn't be happier.

After three years of marriage, our first daughter was born. A really great child. Totally uncomplicated and calm. We were able to travel with her and discovered the most beautiful places in the world as a small family. We thought how nice it would be to bring another child like that into the world. First and foremost, of course, for our daughter, who would then have a little play partner. Our second child, another daughter, is also wonderful, unfortunately not as uncomplicated for a long time. She demanded much more attention and kept us awake for nights on end. Travelling was unfortunately hardly possible with her and not only that suffered, but especially our sex life.

That was previously varied, passionate and, above all, present. And regular!

But of course the many sleepless nights took a lot out of us and once we were in bed we used the quiet time to get some sleep.

In the meantime, both daughters started school and everything improved somewhat. But our sex life has never been as good as it was before. Although we still share many intimate moments, the "special" is somehow missing.

I remember that as students we once saw a documentary about swingers club visitors at night. At first we made fun of it, but after more and more interviews were shown with couples who had already been married to each other for 10 years and were enjoying this irregular kick, we began to imagine what it might be like.

How would it be if we were to leave our children with our parents for the weekend and then get ready for our little "event" in our own house? How I can afford the most beautiful and expensive lingerie in my mid-30s and put it on in front of Thomas and he would love to eat me up already in our bedroom?

How we then excitedly drive into one of the clubs. It has to be tasteful, of course. Not one of those dingy places that are right off a motorway exit. A small, hidden club in a forest perhaps, where the guests all wear eye masks and are dressed very stylishly.

And then I would enter the club on Thomas' arm. The other visitors would look at me and he would enjoy how they all desire me and dream of being allowed to fuck me.

Then he would leave me alone and watch me from afar. I would sit down at the bar and not two minutes later the first man would have already joined me. I would chat with him and then go upstairs with him, into one of the rooms that can be locked but also have windows so other guests can watch.

I'd have my way with the strange man while Thomas stood outside and watched.

I was quite surprised that he was turned on by the thought. I initially thought he wanted a threesome. With another woman. For his sake, I would have gone along with it, but the idea doesn't appeal to me myself. A threesome with another man does. Although I might be a little overwhelmed if I was the center of attention all the time.

The constellation that I have something with a stranger and Thomas is just watching plays into my cards.

We often talked about it until our wedding and thought about it every now and then afterwards. But until today we have never put this fantasy into practice. Something always came in between.

But now the holidays are just around the corner. My parents gave both of our daughters a stay at a horse farm for Christmas. At first, I rolled my eyes. I don't particularly like horses and the prospect of being allowed to accompany my daughters to a horse farm didn't appeal to me very much.

But then my parents said they knew the owners and were happy to be the chaperones who came along.

"While the girls get riding lessons, we go hiking! The scenery there is really gorgeous. If you want, I can also ask for accommodation for you," my mother asked us, but I immediately protested.

Hiking is nice, yes. But the prospect of a childless week is also very nice.

"Remember how we used to fantasize about becoming one of those couples who went to swingers clubs on a regular basis?", I asked Thomas then one night just before the kids' vacation.

Confused, Thomas looked at me. "We imagined this?"

I stand in front of him in our living room and now sit down right next to him on the sofa.

"Yeah ... we were watching this documentary about swingers club visitors at the time. At first we thought it was strange, but then it became more and more charming."

"Really? What exactly did we have in mind?"

I know his memories have come back by now. He wants to hear our shared fantasy from my mouth just once more and I'm happy to go along with it.

I describe everything to him in detail. About the preparations, about my lingerie. Of our arrival at the club and of the stranger.

I can see exactly how Thomas envisions all this, too, and how he likes it.

"I think we should tackle that sometime," he replies to me, smiling.

"I think so too," was my curt reply before I sat down at the laptop to do some research.

It took me a while to find something suitable that met our expectations.

Either they are really dingy clubs, which are located in the middle of the city centre or in the industrial area, or there are parties on exactly that weekend, for which we are already too old with our 35 years.

But then I do track something down. It's a bit further away, but I think that's actually quite good. At least this way we don't run the risk of running into our colleagues or neighbors. That weekend there is also a kind of "masked ball".

While the big evening gown is not expected, a mask is mandatory upon entry. Just what I wanted. On the site's homepage, newcomers are expressly allowed and welcome. And if you wish, you will even be taken by the hand. That would really take away some of my insecurities. An evening in a swingers club is already exciting enough. I don't want to worry about finding all the rooms and behaving correctly. Someone who shows me everything in advance and explains the rules, comes to me just right.

I show the club to Thomas, who nods it off. He's been nervous for days already. Not because he is afraid of what will happen there, but because he is absolutely unsure about the wardrobe. So I've done some research and ordered him a few things. Me too, of course. And it turned out to be really really expensive lingerie. Just like I imagined at the time.

And then, finally, it's time. We said goodbye to our children two days ago and have regular updates from our parents.

There's cell phone ban in the club itself, which is why we can't be notified immediately in case of an emergency. But my parents have planned a visit to the cinema for this evening. What should happen there?

We have already finished the errands for the coming week, cleaned the house and tended the garden and are now in our bedroom.

For Thomas, I chose some tight leather shorts and a black shirt. I even called the club and asked if they would let him in with such an outfit and they assured me that it was absolutely fine.

For me, on the other hand, I have chosen an elaborate set consisting of a corsage with lots of lace and a gossamer panty. In addition, matching nylon stockings, which I can attach to the garters of the corsage. I put the things on and then look at myself in the mirror. Everything really fits perfectly. It's a good thing that I still made sure to exercise regularly after graduation.

I slip on my high heels, the last time I wore them was before I had my first baby, and strut around the bedroom in them.

"Wow," I hear Thomas say, now standing directly in front of me.

I turn around and see his eyes light up. That's exactly how I imagined it. This is how I want him to look at me. I grin, turn and present myself in front of him, enjoying his full attention.

"You look really great. The men will just throw themselves at you," he says.

Then he gets changed as well. Thomas has also always taken care of his body and has not put on a beer belly like many of his friends. Everything still looks just as sporty as before.

He buttons the bottom buttons of his shirt and then looks at himself in the mirror as well.

"We really do make a good couple," he says, hugging me from behind. We exchange a long, tender kiss, but before his hands move under my panties, I push him away from me.

"We should get going," I say firmly. Not that we let this opportunity pass because we couldn't control ourselves.

I put on a long coat and then walk to our car. Thomas has promised to drive so I can have a glass of champagne or two or maybe more. I'm pretty nervous after all and hope that the alcohol will loosen me up a bit.

We have a drive of just under two hours ahead of us and I pray that we don't get caught in the traffic jam. We are already relatively late even now. Not that everything is over when we arrive.

But everything works out fine. We get through without problems and drive up to the gravel parking lot next to the house, which is supposed to be the swingers club. So it says at least the Navi.

"And that's it?", Thomas asks me in wonder.

It looks absolutely inconspicuous. It could also be a restaurant with a guesthouse attached. Or a private compound.

Nothing indicates that inside strangers have sex with each other. But that's exactly how it's supposed to be.

We stay in the car and watch the people parked in front of us. A couple about our age gets out. They are wearing jeans and sneakers and don't look like they are about to go to a swingers club. But then they each get a big bag out of the trunk.

"Do you think they change inside?", Thomas asks me.

"Yeah, definitely. They said to me on the phone that we can bring multiple outfits if we're unsure. There are changing facilities," I reply uncertainly.

"Okay. Shall we go then?" he asks and I take one deep breath. I can feel my heart beating up to my throat. I'm nervous and excited. But I definitely don't want to chicken out now, and I definitely want to see this through to the end. Besides, nothing has to happen in there. If I don't find someone suitable, that's just the way it is.

I talk myself good once again and then follow Thomas, who has also packed a bag as a precaution. With a change of clothes and with comfortable things for the return journey.

We walk the short distance to the door and just see the couple in front of us disappear behind the massive front door.

"Crap. Too late," Thomas mumbles and looks for a bell.

"Chateau Plaisir," he reads on the page, then presses it.

Immediately the door opener sounds and he pushes the door open.

Once again I take a deep breath. Here we go.

We come into a small room. Similar to the anteroom of a village disco. A small table has been set up with a woman behind it, who is still in conversation with the couple in front of us.

"Have fun you guys!" she calls after them as they head down a flight of stairs.

Then it's our turn.

"Hello. Oh ... you're new, aren't you? I haven't seen you here before."

I nod and am glad Thomas is doing the talking.

"Yeah, that's right. My wife had called and told me that you also offer tours for newcomers," he says. The woman nods and beams.

"Yeah yeah. Right. Right. My husband will take the lead. You guys pay me quick, sign the guest list, and then I'll give you a key to the lockers. Then you change down in the basement and come back up and go to the bar. Have a drink there. My husband is out with another group right now... But he'll be with you as soon as he can."

She sounds absolutely nice, which is why I have a good feeling. So we pay, fill in our names and then get handed the key.

Afterwards we go down to the changing rooms and meet the other couple. They are already half naked and instinctively I want to turn around and leave again. After all, this is a co-ed stall and I want to give them some privacy. But Thomas reminds me again where we are. I might even see them completely naked sooner or later.

The woman notices my uncertainty and smiles at me.

"First time?" she asks. I nod.

"Oh ... the first time was so exciting. Wasn't it?" she says, looking at her partner.

"But don't worry. Julian, the owner, will take you by the hand and explain everything. After that, you'll feel ready. I promise."

She turns around so that her partner can close her bra, which is virtually only made of latex bands, on her back. Then she puts on a tiny pair of panties, also made of latex and slips into insanely high patent boots. Wow. I've never seen anything like that in real life.

Her partner also wears skimpy patent panties and heavy boots with numerous buckles. Then they take two blindfolds, also made of latex, out of their pockets and put them on.

"Have fun!" they wish us and then leave the cabin.
54

Speechless I stand still and stow my coat in the closet. Suddenly I feel totally out of place with my lingerie. I dig the mask out of the bag and put it on.

That is already a little better. Thomas is also finished and then we go back upstairs and look for the bar.

We follow the loud music and a little later we find ourselves on a half-full dance floor. The club is already quite well attended and on the sofas sit some men and women.

I look around and realize that there are clearly more men than women here, which I find quite good. So the selection is at least larger for me.

We go to the counter and I feel the first glances on me.

"A water and a glass of champagne," I hear Thomas say as he's ordering for us.

I sip my champagne and see a man, standing all alone on the other side of the room, hold up his wine glass and toast me.

I quickly turn away again.

It's been ages since I've flirted with other men. I don't even know how to do that anymore.

"What's wrong?", Thomas wants to know from me, who noticed me turning around in a panic.

"Nothing. Well, I just didn't think how quickly the men here would make contact," I say after all.

"I'm not surprised at all," he replies with a grin, looking demonstratively at my lingerie.

"You must be the new guys, right?" we are suddenly interrupted.

Again I turn around and see a man around 40 standing in front of us.

"Yeah, right," Thomas responds immediately, shaking his hand.

He looks at me and holds out his hand expectantly.

"Julian. I'm sure my wife at the front has already mentioned me. I'm the owner. I'll give you a little tour in a minute," he explains quickly as I shake his hand and then finish my champagne in one go. I can feel my nervousness getting the better of me and I really need to calm it down.

"Are you ready?" he asks us.

We nod and then follow him.

He shows us the dining room, the wellness area with a sauna and a whirlpool and the "wet area".

"If you want to practice a special fetish, please only here," he says, leaving us confused. But I can already guess what he means by that.

Then we go upstairs where it is much darker. I hear moaning and wonder if the first already have sex here.

"This is our big playground," he says, pointing to a room where several mattresses are laid out on the floor. In the far corner lies a couple who are actually having sex with each other. Whew. How exciting!

He leads us on and we find ourselves in a dark room with several levels.

"If you like to have sex and would rather just be heard doing it or listen to others doing it," he says, pointing to the reclining areas on each floor where a maximum of two people can fit. You can barely see anything unless you're standing at the same height, but you could actually hear everything.

We move on and find ourselves in a completely dark room.

"Our darkroom," is all he says, pointing to the dark room.

"When your eyes adjust to the darkness, you can make out a few outlines. But nothing more."

We continue and reach a room with a cage.

"You can lock the cage from the inside," Julian explains. "So you can watch, but you can't participate."

I imagine myself in this cage... With a stranger. And how Thomas has to stand in front of it and watch me while I have sex with the stranger. Whew ... the nervousness is slowly saying goodbye and being replaced by excitement. I can hardly wait to finally get started.

We take a look at another room. There is a large play area here as well.

"Anyone who goes in here automatically agrees that they are willing to have sex with others. After asking first, of course," says Julian.

"And there are a couple of individual rooms up ahead. With a gyn chair, with a massage table or with a bed. All of them can't be seen and are lockable," he explains as he passes by.

Then we'll go back down.

"And now for the rules of conduct. No means no. If someone pushes your hand away, that also means no.

If someone closes the door, that doesn't mean you have to keep knocking to check if they might want viewers.

Drinks and food only downstairs. No clothes in the sauna and smoking only outside. Mhh...anything else? Oh yeah. Put towels underneath when you go to the play area. There are fresh ones everywhere.

Have fun!" he finally says and waits for a reaction from us. Thomas and I look at each other. We have to let that sink in first.

"No questions?"

We shake our heads.

"Wonderful. "

He turns around and walks towards the entrance. Probably to greet the next ones.

Indecisive we remain standing. Where to go first?

"Want to go see something?" asks Thomas, and relieved, I nod.

But first I need another glass of wine or champagne. We go back to the bar and I quickly empty another glass. I really need more courage to pull this off right away. Thomas lets his gaze wander through the crowd.

"So, anyone you could see yourself doing that with yet?" he asks me. I follow his gaze and look at the men. Most of them are our age. Maybe a few years older, some younger. I see one man who actually stands out a bit from the crowd. He's here alone, wearing only a tight pair of boxers. Nothing else. But because of that you can see his trained upper body very well. He's younger than us. Maybe mid 20's or so and I can see he's attracting the attention of the other couples as well. Everyone is looking at him and whispering. He's going to have sex today for sure.

"That one," I say, pointing at the young man before another couple beats me to it.

"Oh ... the boy? Really?", Thomas asks in amazement, but then he grins.

He leaves me alone at the bar and walks towards the man. Suddenly I'm all excited. What is he doing now?

I watch him and watch as he talks to the stranger. Then they turn around and Thomas points at me. Oh man. How awkward. The stranger smiles at me and then nods.

He seems okay with it. But with what? Talking to me? Getting to know me? Having sex with me?

He comes to me with the stranger and introduces us.

"This is Tim. And this is Anne, my wife," he says.

Tim is still smiling and then holds out his hand to me, which I shake a little shyly.

"Another glass of wine?", Thomas asks me, pointing to my empty glass.

Eagerly, I nod.

He disappears all the way to the other end of the bar, leaving me with Tim, who starts a conversation with me. He wants to know if it's my first time here and what I hope to experience here.

I gather all my courage and tell him about our plan. That I want to have sex with a strange man while my own is watching.

Tim nods.

"Agreed," he says suddenly, reaching for my hand.

He leads me out of the bar and then leaves me standing in the hallway all at once.

"Hold on," he says, and I see him hurry back to the counter, where Thomas is still standing. He whispers something to him, who just nods eagerly and then gives up on ordering anything else. I see him stop for a moment and give Tim a bit of a head start before following us.

"Does he know where we're going?", I ask in a panic. If we're about to have sex, Thomas definitely needs to know where we are.

"Yeah, he'll find us," he says, pulling me up to the first floor. There he stops in the middle of the hallway and pushes me against the wall. His hands are on my body, running over my waist and down my legs.

I feel his left hand on my ass and his hot breath on my neck. Then he looks at me and we kiss.

It feels good. It's the first time I've kissed another man in years. It's so new and so strange. And yet so exciting at the same time. I close my eyes and let myself go completely into the kiss until he lets go of me again and moves on.

I look around and can see Thomas standing behind us, slowly following us.

He doesn't look jealous or angry. On the contrary. He nods encouragingly at me and I can see how much that excites him.

We go into one of the smaller rooms. There is only one bed in there and otherwise it is empty.

Tim kisses me again and pushes me against the wall again. His kisses are a little more demanding and passionate this time. I feel his cock pressing against my crotch and how it gets harder and thicker.

I slowly block out everything around me. That I just met Tim a few minutes ago. That I'm in a swingers club. That any second my husband or other spectators could be in the room watching me very closely.

Then Tim pulls me away from the wall and pushes me onto the bed. Back first I land on it and briefly glance at the door. Thomas is standing there watching us. But he's not the only one. More men are standing next to him and are also looking over at us.

I try to focus on Tim again, who wanders his face down my body. He kisses me over my stomach, over my legs and then spreads them.

Slowly, he slides the panties off my hips and runs his fingers through my wet cleft.

Mhh ... how good that feels. I am already all day a mixture of nervous and excited. This morning I woke up thinking that I could have sex with a strange man in the evening and now it's finally happening. I close my eyes and concentrate fully on his fingers.

They gently drive through my pussy, searching for my clit and begin to rub it.

I groan softly. Oh, how good that feels.

He continues, lets his fingers wander deeper to my wet hole and starts to play with it. He rubs over it and then penetrates me deeply with one finger. I can not help but sigh loudly and notice how the men come closer to see and hear better.

Tim adds another finger. Oh, yeah. He fucks me with it. First very slowly, then harder and faster.

I feel a tickle on my thighs and blink my eyes. I see him with his face very close to my pussy. And then I feel it. His tongue. Licking ever so gently over my clit. Oh wow. How incredible that feels. His fingers inside me. His tongue on my pearl.

He continues. Fucks me with his fingers and licks me at the same time.

I dig my fingers into the sheets. It won't be long before I cum.

By now I have completely blocked out where I am, and have stopped noticing that a few men are standing around me and watching very closely what is happening.

Once again I close my eyes and let myself go fully into the beautiful feeling and then I come.

I moan out my lust loudly, arch my upper body upwards and then tear my eyes open. The men stand around the bed and some have meanwhile unpacked their cocks to jerk off on me. Thomas is standing among them, watching me closely. A grin has formed on his face, which I return.

Then I turn around and stretch my ass towards Tim. I want to feel his spanking inside me now.

He understands immediately and I feel his hands on my hips. Then I look up and see Thomas standing right in front of me. He must have changed places.

I hold his gaze as Tim slides his cock through my wet crack, looking right at him as he enters me.

Oh, what a horny feeling to feel this younger man inside me while my own husband watches.

I watch him jerk his cock while a strange man fucks me.

It feels so good to come back another time.

Tim comes too and I don't even notice how he slowly lets go of me and leaves me alone on the mat. The other men are still standing around us.

I look at Thomas questioningly, but he just nods at me. I grin and look at the men.

There's one I like quite a bit. A little older than me, athletic, gray temples, nice face. He returns my smile and joins me on the bed. The other men also want to join me, but Thomas stops them.

He has already unwrapped his cock. He is big, thick and hard. I take it in my hand and run my fingers up and down with pleasure. It feels good to hold a different one than my husband's in my hand again. And it's even hornier when he's standing right in front of you and watching.

I let my hand slide up and down, then bend down to him.
I can see the first drops of pleasure on his tip and then lick them off with my tongue.

And once I've had a taste, I take his cock completely in my mouth. I hear not only the moaning from the stranger, but also from Thomas, who continues to watch excitedly.

Passionately I suck the foreign beating, push him deep into my mouth and work him in between again and again with my hand, until I turn around another time to make it clear to him that he should fuck me now.

I position myself again so that Thomas can look directly at me and let my lust out even louder and more violently this time.

I never thought I would enjoy it so much.

I cum one more time before the stranger comes as well, splashing me on the back and leaving me alone on the mattress one more time.

Thomas is standing right in front of me and I want to pull him to me, but he blocks. Instead, he points to the other men in the room. He would like to see me with them.

So I choose another one to lick me and bring me to another climax before another man fucks me properly again.

But then I've had enough. I get up, chase the rest of the men out of the room and grab my husband.

I close the door behind us and lie back on the bed.

"Fuck me! ", I say to him, who has been on the verge of a climax every now and then, but then held back at the last moment.

He joins me on the bed, guides his cock to my pussy and penetrates me.

With fast and well-directed thrusts he fucks me before he comes loudly and quite violently and squirts his whole load in my face. I am maximally excited and run my finger around my mouth, which is now full of cum and lick it off.

Then I lie down with my husband, hold him tight, feel the sweat on his skin and how fast his heart beats. He really held back the climax for a long time and I really wanted to experience it with him.

We wait a brief moment, exchanging another long, passionate kiss before opening the door again and driving away the curious men behind it.

"Will there be more later?" one of the men asks us hopefully. He has just not made his move.

"Maybe," Thomas replies curtly, and then pulls me with him into the nearest bathroom, where we undress and take a long shower first.

Afterwards we go back downstairs and help ourselves to the rich buffet.

As we munch on the good home cooking, we look around again.
The couples here seem happy, exuberant and so open.

I look at Thomas, who drops down next to me with a fully loaded plate. He looks happy as well.
68

"Do we come here often?", I ask him.

Briefly, he looks at me in confusion. But then he nods eagerly, "Absolutely!"

I return his smile and then turn my attention to my potatoes before casting my gaze around the dining room and catching sight of a man smiling at me as soon as our eyes crossed.

I'm rushing to eat because I can't wait to get right back upstairs ...

About the man
who knows what he wants

Completely drenched in sweat, I get off Ralph and roll over onto my stomach. Whew. That was awesome. We just had our third date and I was prepared for it to end today with me or with him, but I'd never have dreamed for it to turn out so good!

His hands are just magical. And his mouth!

Even as we left the restaurant, I could tell it wasn't just going to be a goodbye kiss. He was more demanding this time, more impatient. And I let myself get carried away. Made out with him on the street and giggled as passers by looked at us funny. No wonder. His hand slid up my skirt within a few seconds each time. Right to my ass.

And then we went to my place because it was closer.

We were too impatient to wait for the elevator and took the stairs. On each floor we stopped to kiss and each time we had one less piece of clothing on. And then, finally, we were in my apartment. The door slammed shut and then after five seconds I was completely naked.

Stumbling backwards I pulled him into my bedroom and within a few hours experienced three incredible orgasms. First he licked me, then spoiled with his fingers and finally I rode him until we came together.

First time sex has never worked so well with anyone.

"Are you okay?" he asks me, putting his hand on my back and starting to stroke me. Whew ... those hands. They're so big, so manly, and so gentle at the same time. A pretty good mix, if you ask me.

"Sure," I say, turning my head in his direction. His brown hair is a little disheveled from reaching in with my fingers so many times. There's a fine film of sweat on his body. He really put a lot of effort into pleasuring me. Finally, someone who puts value on it.

"How about a massage?" he then asks me. Oh ... now he wants to charge me for it. I should have guessed.

"What do you want to get massaged?"

"No, no. Do you want one?"

Seriously? First he gets me so good and then he wants to massage me? I can hardly believe my luck and nod enthusiastically. He asks for massage oil and I point to the small drawer in my bedside cabinet, where there are also lubricants and condoms.

I lie down on my stomach, clear all the pillows and the disturbing blanket aside and rest my head on the flat of my hands.

Then I close my eyes and feel the first drops of massage oil land on my back.

Ralph spreads the oil on my skin with his big hands and sits next to me. It really feels good how he kneads me sometimes gently and then sometimes a little harder.

He spreads the oil now also on my legs, massages my calves and my feet. Then he wanders higher again until he has arrived at my buttocks, to which he devotes himself particularly intensively. Again and again he runs his hands over it and then suddenly lands with his fingers in my butt fold.

Mhh ... what a pleasant feeling that is. He hears how I moan comfortably and spreads some more oil on me. Again he massages my ass and I feel how the liquid oil flows through my crack and lands on my pussy. With his fingers he catches the oil and spreads it. On me and also a little inside me.

My lust rises immediately. His fingers at this point feel great.

With his fingertips he penetrates my warm pussy while his other hand is on my butt. Then his fingers move further upwards. Drive again through my butt fold and then pause at my relaxed hole. He circles it, moistens it with the oil and plays with it.

Again, I groan. The feeling is nice too, although I'm not really a big fan of it otherwise. But Ralph does it so well and so gently that I can really enjoy it.

He now changes his sitting position and pushes my legs a little apart so that he can sit between them.

He lets some oil drip on it and then very slowly and carefully pushes a fingertip into me. The feeling almost drives me crazy. It feels so pleasant and so good. I did not know that yet, but so far it is just horny.

He slides his finger deeper and plays with my clit with his other hand. He rubs and teases it while his finger is still in my ass.

Now he starts to move it. Very carefully he pulls it out and then pushes it back in. Until it becomes easier and easier.

I notice how I relax more and more. How I become more ready for more. Ralph notices this too, which is why he takes another finger with him.

Very carefully and gently he pushes it with his other finger into my once so tight hole, which expands further and further.

I groan another time. Mhh ... how good that feels.

He moves his fingers. Twists them a little, pulls them out and pushes them back in.

His hand continues to rest on my pussy and I feel him press fingers into my warm, wet hole there as well.

By now I don't even know where up and down is. It all feels so wet and so humid. So warm and so hot. Are there now more fingers in my pussy or in my ass? Which hand is he using to work my clit? I don't know. But it feels good and I can feel my lust rising more and more.

I notice him pull one hand away again and place it against my legs. He pulls them up so that my ass goes up while my face continues to lie flat on my hands. So he gets even better access to everything.

His hand goes back to my pussy, stroking and rubbing my clit while two of his fingers continue deep in my ass. He starts moving them again. Thrusts them in and out. Spreads them to make even more room inside me. For more fingers or for his cock?

I notice myself getting looser and looser and moan out loud when I notice another finger on my ass. Carefully he pushes it into his other fingers and stretches me more and more.

I am now completely uninhibited. Moan out my lust, push my ass towards him so that he can press his fingers deep inside me.

He straightens up now. Kneels next to me and holds me with one hand on the back, while his other hand is busy with my ass. Harder and harder he now fucks my ass with his three fingers and I feel how I'm about to experience an intense orgasm.

Again he moves. This time he kneels between my legs again. I feel something hard against my thighs. Is that his cock, which is already aroused again?

His deft fingers speed up even more and I feel his bulging spanking against my pussy. He lets it slide once through my wet cleft until he pushes it into me without warning.

Oh, wow. What an intense feeling that is.

His fingers are still inside my ass, making me even tighter.

I feel his cock more intense and better than before and almost go insane with lust when he starts fucking me with it. He thrusts properly while he continues to keep his fingers in my ass, moving them briefly every now and then.

Then he pauses. Is he going to fuck me in the ass now? I hope so.

He pulls back his cock and his fingers as well. With his thumb he runs over my stretched hole, moistens it once again with my own juice and then I feel his bulging glans against my tight hole.

Gently, he pushes it in. Oh man. What a horny feeling as he slowly drills into my ass and then the thick shaft follows. Such a cock is rather more than a few fingers.

Very slowly he lets the rest follow and again I moan with pleasure as I feel his whole spanking inside me.

His hand goes to my clit and starts rubbing it while he starts fucking me in the ass. First very slowly and then faster and harder.

I can feel the next orgasm coming on.

My body tenses and my fingers claw as if automatically into the bed sheet. Only a few more pushes and I come.

And then the time has come. Loudly I let out my climax and enjoy the last, intense thrusts that follow until he also comes loudly in my ass.

Then he drops down next to me on the bed.

He pulls me to him and I can feel his heart beating hard as his breathing slowly calms down.

"Feeling good?" he asks me, and eagerly I nod.

I lay in his arms while his hand runs over my bottom over and over again until we eventually fall asleep.

Printed in Great Britain
by Amazon